DATE DUE			
JAN 2 7 2005	FEB 28 2007		
	MAR 16 2007		
DEC 21 2005	APR 19 2007		
	DEC 8 2008		
DEC 4 2006	MAR 10 2009		
DEC 15 2005	NOV 05 2010		
JAN 16 2007	NOV 28 2011		
JAN 22 2007			

797.3
VOE

T 32990
Voeller, Edward A.

Extreme surfin

Extreme Surfing

by Edward Voeller

Consultant:
Linda M. Theurer
Assistant to Competition Director
United States Surfing Federation (USSF)

CAPSTONE BOOKS
an imprint of Capstone Press
Mankato, Minnesota

Capstone Books are published by Capstone Press
151 Good Counsel Drive, P.O. Box 669, Mankato, Minnesota 56002
http://www.capstone-press.com

Library of Congress Cataloging-in-Publication Data
Voeller, Edward A.
    Extreme surfing/by Edward Voeller.
    p. cm.—(Extreme sports)
    Includes bibliographical references and index.
    Summary: Describes the history of surfing and the equipment, skills, techniques,
and safety concerns of this sport.
    ISBN 0-7368-0485-4
    1. Surfing—Juvenile literature. 2. Extreme sports—Juvenile literature.
[1. Surfing.] I. Title. II. Series.

GV840.S8 V64 2000
797.3'2—dc21   99-047919

Editorial Credits
Carrie A. Braulick, editor; Timothy Halldin, cover designer; Kia Bielke, production
    designer and illustrator; Heidi Schoof, photo researcher

Photo Credits
Archive Photos, 11
International Stock, 4, 16; International Stock/Robert Brown, 24, 38
John S. Callahan/Photo Resource Hawaii, cover, 41
L. Paul Mann/Mercury Press, 7, 13, 37
Photo Network/Scott Winer, 30; Darrell Jones, 46
Transparencies, Inc./Jane Faircloth, 14
Unicorn Stock Photos, 8, 20, 22; Unicorn Stock Photos/Scott Liles, 28
Uniphoto/Randy Napier, 19
Waverly Traylor, 26, 34, 43

Table of Contents

Chapter One

Extreme Surfing

Extreme surfing is a sport in which people ride surfboards on large waves. Extreme surfers usually surf in the ocean. They perform stunts while they surf. They may do spins on waves. They may perform stunts in the air. Extreme surfers often compete in surfing competitions.

Waves

Extreme surfers look for the best waves to ride. Surfers ride waves that are starting to break near the shore. Waves that break turn into foamy water called white water. Surfers

Extreme surfers perform stunts on waves in the ocean.

call white water "soup." Extreme surfers often ride waves called swells. These waves have long, continuous crests.

Extreme surfers sometimes travel long distances to find the best waves. Hawaii is one of the most popular surfing locations. The Pacific Ocean off the coast of Hawaii has large swells for surfers to ride. Surfers surf off North American coasts in the Pacific and Atlantic Oceans. Surfers also ride large waves in the Atlantic Ocean off European and African coasts.

Riding Waves

Surfers lie on their boards and paddle out toward breaking waves to begin surfing. They then wait for a large wave. They sometimes sit on their boards to get a better view of the waves. Surfers face the shore when a wave they want to ride comes toward them. They then stand on their surfboards and ride the wave. This is called "catching a wave." Surfers paddle their surfboards out into deeper water

Waves turn into white water after they break.

again after the wave breaks near shore. They
then find another good wave to catch.

Surfers balance on their surfboards as
they ride waves. They crouch on their boards
and put their hands out to keep their balance.
Surfers keep their feet apart. This keeps their
weight evenly balanced over their boards.
Surfers move their feet and shift their body
weight to turn.

Chapter Two

History

No one knows exactly when surfing began. Historians say that people surfed more than 1,000 years ago. These people lived on the Polynesian Islands in the Pacific Ocean. They pushed heavy wooden surfboards out into the ocean. The boards were as long as 20 feet (6 meters) and weighed about 150 pounds (70 kilograms). Islanders then rode the boards back to shore.

James Cook was an English sea captain. He sailed to what is now the Hawaiian islands in 1778. He found that surfing was a popular sport on the islands. Hawaiian surfers used

Surfing's popularity has increased during the past 1,000 years.

wooden boards that were about 18 feet (5 meters) long. Cook described these surfers in reports about his trip to Hawaii.

Surfing Superstar

Duke Kahanamoku was the first famous surfer. He organized the first surfing club. He also was the first surfer elected to the Surfing Hall of Fame.

Kahanamoku was born in Honolulu, Hawaii, in 1890. As a child, he became an expert swimmer. He also was an excellent surfer. Kahanamoku surfed on a long, heavy surfboard made of wood. He could surf backward and perform headstands on his surfboard. He also gave rides to friends on the board.

In 1912, Kahanamoku broke a world swimming record and won a gold medal in the Olympic Games. That year, the games were held in Stockholm, Sweden. Kahanamoku stopped in California on the way to Sweden. He surfed on the Pacific Ocean. People who saw him surf were impressed by his abilities.

Duke Kahanamoku was an excellent swimmer and surfer.

Kahanamoku introduced surfing to the world. After the Olympics, he performed swimming and surfing demonstrations in Europe and the United States. In 1915, Kahanamoku demonstrated surfing in Australia. Many people gathered on beaches to watch his demonstrations.

New Surfboards

After Kahanamoku's demonstrations, people throughout the world became interested in surfing. But not everyone could surf. Wooden surfboards were long and heavy. They also were slow and difficult to move in the water.

In 1926, a surfer named Tom Blake made the first hollow, wooden surfboards. These lightweight boards were faster and easier to move than solid boards. Many people tried surfing with these boards. In 1935, Blake added a fin called a skeg to the bottom of the boards. This helped surfers control their boards. Modern surfboards have three skegs.

In the 1940s, surfboard manufacturers began to use foam and fiberglass to make surfboards. Fiberglass is a strong, light material made of woven glass fibers. These surfboards were lighter and easier to handle than the hollow, wooden surfboards. More people began to surf using these boards.

Today's surfboards are made of foam and fiberglass.

Surfing's Popularity Increases

Surfing's popularity increased during the 1960s. In 1964, the first World Surfing Championships were held in Sydney, Australia. Many people formed surfing organizations in the 1960s. Members of these organizations surfed together. They also competed in surfing competitions.

Some organizations set rules and standards for surfing competitions. Today, the International Surfing Association (ISA) governs surfing events throughout the world. The ISA organizes competitions and sets world surfing guidelines. The United States Surfing Federation (USSF) governs competitive surfing in the United States.

Many surfers test their skills in competitions.

Chapter Three
Equipment and Safety

Surfers must have proper surfing equipment. They make sure their equipment is in good condition. Surfers also follow safety measures.

Surfboards

Surfers can choose to use short or long boards. Both types of surfboards are made of fiberglass and foam. Competitive surfers often use short boards. Short boards are 5 to 7 feet (1.5 to 2.1 meters) long. Short boards usually have a pointed nose. The nose is the front of a surfboard. This makes short boards easy to move. Most short boards weigh less than 25 pounds

Short boards usually have pointed noses.

(11 kilograms). Short boards allow surfers to easily perform difficult moves and stunts.

Most beginning surfers ride long boards. Long boards are 8 to 10 feet (2.4 to 3 meters) long. Long boards usually have a rounded nose. This helps keep the boards steady.

Long boards are more stable than short boards. This makes them easier to balance on waves. Long boards also ride smoother on rough water. But long boards are more difficult to turn and move. This makes it difficult to perform stunts on long boards. Some surfing competitions have special competitions for surfers who ride long boards.

Other Equipment

Surfers also use other equipment when they surf. They wear an ankle leash. These elastic cords are about 7 feet (2 meters) long. Surfers attach one end of the leash to an ankle. They attach the other end to the

Ankle leashes keep surfers connected to their boards.

surfboard. Ankle leashes prevent surfboards from floating too far away from surfers after they wipe out. Surfers who wipe out fall off their boards.

Many surfers wear wet suits to stay warm in cold water. These rubber suits allow a thin layer of water to enter between a surfer's skin and the suit. The surfer's body heat warms the water. This keeps the surfer warm. Surfers who

do not wear wet suits may get hypothermia. This condition occurs when a person's body temperature becomes too low. It can cause death.

Surfers also use other supplies. They apply wax to the deck of their boards. Surfers stand on a board's deck. Wax helps surfers' feet grip the boards. Some surfers use track pads. Surfers put these pads on the back of their boards. This helps surfers position their back foot on the boards to make sharp turns.

Safety

Safe surfers learn about an area before they enter the water. They surf at locations where there are no dangerous reefs. The ocean floor rises in these areas near the shore. Surfers who fall off their boards near reefs may hit their head on the ocean floor. Surfers also make sure sharks are not in the area. Sharks sometimes attack people in the water. Surfers also make sure the area is not used for swimming or boating. Surfers who surf in these areas may

Wet suits keep surfers warm in cold water.

crash into swimmers or boats. Surfers can ask lifeguards or other surfers whether an area is safe for surfing.

Surfers follow other safety measures to prevent accidents and injuries. Many surfers use sunblock. This lotion helps prevent surfers from becoming sunburned. Safe surfers always surf with a partner. A partner can help a surfer who wipes out. Surfers wait their turn to catch waves in crowded surfing areas. They do not surf too closely to other surfers. This helps surfers avoid accidents.

Surfers stay away from their boards when they wipe out. They try to fall off the back or sides of their boards. This helps prevent them from getting hit by their boards.

Surfers who wipe out try to fall off the back of their boards.

Ankle Leash

Deck

Skeg

Surfboard

Wet Suit

Nose

Chapter Four
Skills

Surfers need a variety of skills. They must be strong swimmers. It takes a great deal of strength and energy to paddle out to waves. Surfers also should have good balance. They must be able to keep their boards steady on breaking waves.

Paddling

Surfers must learn certain skills to help them paddle out to waves. Surfers need to keep their boards flat when they paddle. They balance on the boards to keep the boards stable.

Surfers balance on their surfboards as they ride waves.

Surfers lie on their boards and paddle with their arms to reach breaking waves.

Surfers sometimes must paddle through large waves. Surfers paddle directly into these waves. Some surfers wrap their legs around the board. They move their weight forward on the board. The board's nose then dips under the water. The waves then roll over the surfers. This move is called a duck dive.

Catching a Wave

Surfers follow several steps to catch a wave. They paddle toward shore when they see a large wave moving toward them. They use their arms to push their body up higher when the wave rises under them. They then swing their legs under their body and stand on their boards.

Most surfers stand on their surfboards with their left foot forward. Other surfers stand with their right foot forward. These surfers are using a goofy-foot stance.

Beginning surfers should practice catching waves. They often ride on soup after waves break. Soup is easier to catch than large waves. Beginners also may practice in artificial wave pools. The waves in these pools usually are only about 2 feet (.5 meter) high. Beginners can learn how to balance on these small waves.

Angling and Turning

Most waves break gradually from left to right as surfers face the shore. Surfers angle their boards in the direction in which a wave is breaking. They ride the wave just below the

wave's crest. This area of the wave is called the pocket. Surfers stay just ahead of the breaking wave in the pocket.

Surfers may perform leaning or rear foot turns as they ride waves. Surfers lean and shift their weight to perform leaning turns. To turn left, surfers shift their weight to the heels of their feet. To turn right, surfers shift their weight to the balls of their feet.

Surfers perform rear foot turns differently than leaning turns. Surfers shift their weight to their front foot to do rear foot turns. They move their rear foot slightly back. To turn left, they place their rear foot near the left side of the board. To turn right, they place their rear foot near the right side of the board.

Surfers sometimes move into the wave's trough. This long, narrow channel is in the low area between two waves. Surfers then perform a cutback to get out of the trough. They turn and go back up to the pocket to perform this move. Surfers lean in the direction of the turn. They move their rear foot farther back on the

Surfers lean and shift their weight to perform leaning turns.

Surfing Slang

barrel or tube wave—a wave that rolls forward at the top and forms a tunnel

bomb—a large wave that appears suddenly

choppy wave—a wave with little form that breaks in various places

clean face—a face with a smooth surface

cloudbreaker—a wave that breaks far from shore

cranking wave—a large wave that breaks quickly on a zipper

face—the side of a wave that faces the shore

gnarly wave—a wild, rough wave; gnarly waves often are difficult and dangerous to surf.

grinder—a large barrel or tube wave

mushy wave—a weak wave

peeler—a wave that curls as it breaks

rippled face—a face with a rough surface

wedge—a steep wave

zipper—a series of waves that break quickly

surfboard. Surfers then shift their weight to the front of the board.

Daring Surfers

Some extreme surfers are not satisfied with surfing on waves near the shore. These surfers go out into deeper parts of the ocean to surf. Waves in deep ocean water are larger than waves near shore. Some of these waves are more than 50 feet (15 meters) high. People on jet skis often pull surfers into waves in deep ocean water. Jet skis are small watercraft powered by engines. This is called "towing-in." Surfers hang onto a tow rope attached to the jet skis. They let go of the rope and surf when they enter the waves.

Most surfers do not surf on waves in deep ocean water. These waves are too large and powerful for many surfers to catch. The waves also are dangerous. They may hold surfers under water after surfers wipe out.

Chapter Five
Competition

Extreme surfing competitions are popular throughout the world. Many of these competitions are off the coast of Hawaii. Competitive surfers perform stunts to score points. Some surfers are amateurs. These surfers usually do not compete for prize money. Other surfers are professionals. These surfers receive prize money for winning at competitions.

Professional surfers often have sponsors. These sponsors usually are large companies that sell surfboards or surfing equipment. Surfers display sponsors' names or logos on their clothing or equipment. Some surfers use their sponsors'

Competitive surfers may be either amateurs or professionals.

equipment. In return, sponsors pay for some of surfers' travel expenses, equipment costs, or entry fees.

Surfing Stunts

Extreme surfers perform a variety of stunts at competitions. They may perform an off-the-lip move. Surfers glide off a wave's crest to perform this move. They hold the edge of their surfboard in the air. They then turn around in mid-air to get back on the wave.

Surfers also may perform tube rides. The crests of some large waves curl forward to form tubes. Surfers ride the waves inside the tubes.

The floater is another stunt surfers perform. Surfers perform this stunt by surfing up the front of a wave and over its crest. They ride on the wave's back. Surfers then turn around. They surf back over the crest and down the wave's front.

Scoring

Contest judges award surfers points based on the stunts surfers perform. They award surfers who perform difficult stunts more points. The

Competitive surfers sometimes perform tube rides.

surfer with the most points at the end of a competition wins.

Judges watch surfers through binoculars from shore. Binoculars allow judges to closely observe the surfers. Judges look for good turns, cutbacks, off-the-lip moves, floaters, and other stunts. They also judge surfers on style. Surfers' stunts should be smooth, fast, and powerful. Judges watch how surfers balance. Surfers who flap their arms show poor balance. Judges may give fewer points to these surfers. They give no points to surfers who wipe out during a move.

Judges also award points for the type of waves surfers ride. Surfers must choose their waves carefully. They need large waves to perform their moves smoothly. Large waves also allow surfers to perform a greater number of stunts before the waves break. Surfers receive points for the size and shape of the waves they catch.

Judges watch where surfers ride waves. Surfers try to get in the pocket of large, powerful waves. These surfers may earn more points.

Surfers try to catch large, powerful waves during competitions.

World Surfing Games

Thirty-four countries currently participate in the World Surfing Games. This event takes place every two years. The ISA organizes this amateur competition.

Surfers must be members of national teams to participate in the World Surfing Games. The USSF chooses surfers for the United States National Surfing Team. This team represents the United States at the World Surfing Games and other international surfing competitions.

Other Competitions

The National Scholastic Surfing Association (NSSA) organizes many amateur surfing events in the United States each year. Many of these contests are for students.

Professional surfers compete in the World Championship Tour. The Association of Surfing Professionals (ASP) conducts this series of competitions. The surfer with the most points at the end of the year is the professional surfing champion.

Professional surfers also compete in the U.S. Open of Surfing. This competition is one of the

Surfing competitions are popular throughout the world.

largest professional surfing competitions in
the world. More than 700 surfers compete
in this event.

Surfing competitions are popular throughout
the world. Extreme surfers continue to look
for new ways to challenge themselves. They
ride larger waves. They practice new surfing
stunts. They show their improved skills
during competitions.

Words to Know

crest (KREST)—the top of a wave

fiberglass (FYE-bur-glass)—a strong, light material made of woven glass fibers

hypothermia (hye-puh-THUR-mee-uh)—a condition in which a person's body temperature becomes too low

pocket (POK-it)—the area just below a wave's crest; surfers try to stay in the pocket when they surf.

skeg (SKEG)—a fin on the bottom of the back of a surfboard; skegs help surfers control their boards.

soup (SOOP)—the white, foamy water a wave forms after it breaks

swell (SWEL)—a large wave with a long, continuous crest

trough (TRAWF)—the low point between two waves

To Learn More

Bizley, Kirk. *Surfing.* Radical Sports.
Des Plaines, Ill.: Heinemann Library, 1999.

Brimner, Larry Dane. *Surfing.* A First Book.
New York: Franklin Watts, 1997.

Gutman, Bill. *Surfing.* Action Sports.
Minneapolis: Capstone Books, 1995.

Holden, Phil. *Wind and Surf.* All Action.
Minneapolis: Lerner Publications, 1992.

You can read more about surfing in *Surfer* and
Surfing Magazine publications.

Useful Addresses

International Surfing Association
5580 La Jolla Boulevard
Suite 145
La Jolla, CA 92037

International Surfing Museum
411 Olive Avenue
Huntington Beach, CA 92648

National Scholastic Surfing Association
P.O. Box 495
Huntington Beach, CA 92648

United States Surfing Federation
P.O. Box 1070
Virginia Beach, VA 23451

Internet Sites

ASPLive Home Page
http://www.asplive.com

International Surfing Association (ISA)
http://www.isa-wsg.org/index.html

National Scholastic Surfing Association (NSSA)
http://www.nssa.org/frameset.htm

New School Surfing
http://www.geocities.com/Colosseum/Track/5378

The Santa Cruz Surfing Museum
http://www.cruzio.com/arts/scva/surf.html

United States Surfing Federation (USSF)
http://www.ussurf.org

Index